LITTLE RED RIDING HOOD

FSC

Mixed Sources
Product group from well-managed
forests and other controlled sources

Cert no. BV-COC-070303
www.fsc.org
© 1996 Forest Stewardship Council

First published in the United States, Great Britain, Canada, Australia, and New Zealand in 2009
by North-South Books Inc., an imprint of NordSüd Verlag AG, CH-8005 Zürich, Switzerland.
Distributed in the United States by North-South Books Inc., New York 10001.

Typography by Christy Hale

Library of Congress Cataloging-in-Publication Data is available.
ISBN: 978-0-7358-2256-6 (trade edition).
10 9 8 7 6 5 4 3 2 1
Printed in Belgium

www.northsouth.com

LITTLE RED RIDING HOOD

The Brothers Grimm • illustrated by Bernadette Watts

NorthSouth
New York / London

Once upon a time, there was a little girl who was loved by all who knew her, but especially by her grandmother. Grandmother had given the child a red velvet hood, and the little girl loved it so much that she would never wear anything else. And so she got the nickname Red Riding Hood.

One day her mother said to her, "Little Red Riding Hood, take this cake and bottle of cordial to Grandmother. She is not feeling well, and they will do her good. But promise me you won't stray from the path. Walk straight to Grandmother's and be sure to say good morning when you get there."

Little Red Riding Hood promised and set out with her basket.

Grandmother lived in the woods, a half hour's walk from the village. As Little Red Riding Hood walked along, she saw a wolf in front of her on the path. She had never met a wolf before, so she was not a bit afraid.

"Good morning, Red Riding Hood," he said.

"Good morning, Wolf," she answered, remembering to be polite.

"Where might you be going on this fine day?" the wolf asked.

"To Grandmother's house," Red Riding Hood told him. "She has not been feeling well."

"And what do you have in your basket?" asked the wolf.

"Some cake and some cordial," said Red Riding Hood, "to make her feel better."

"Where does your grandmother live?" the wolf wanted to know.
"A bit farther into the woods," Red Riding Hood told him,
"straight down this path."

"Hmmmm," thought the wolf. "This little girl will make a tasty treat indeed, much more tender than the old woman. I will have the old woman for dinner and this little morsel for dessert."

The wolf walked a little way with Red Riding Hood. Then he said, "Look at all the lovely flowers! I am sure your grandmother would love to have some."

Red Riding Hood looked at all the bright flowers dancing in the woods. "What a perfect gift for Grandmother," she thought. "It is still early. I have plenty of time to pick a nice bouquet."

So Little Red Riding Hood left the path to pick the flowers.
But each time she picked one, she saw another a little farther on,
and so she wandered deeper and deeper into the woods.

Meanwhile, the wolf went straight to Grandmother's cottage and knocked on the door.

"Who is it?" called Grandmother.

"It is Red Riding Hood," said the wolf in the sweetest voice he could manage.

"Lift the latch and come in, my dear," said Grandmother. "I am too weak to get out of bed."

The wolf lifted the latch, sprang through the door, and swallowed the poor old woman whole. Then he put on her gown and nightcap, climbed into her bed, and drew the curtains.

When Red Riding Hood had picked all the flowers she could carry, she hurried on to Grandmother's house. She was surprised to see the door standing open.

"Good morning, Grandmother," she called from the doorway, but no one answered. So she walked over to the bed and opened the curtains. There lay her grandmother; but she had pulled her nightcap around her face, and she looked very odd.

"Oh, Grandmother," said Red Riding Hood, "what big ears you have."

"The better to hear you with, my dear," said the wolf.

"Oh, Grandmother, what big eyes you have!"

"The better to see you with," said the wolf.

"Oh, Grandmother, what big teeth you have," said Red Riding Hood.

"The better to EAT you with, my dear!" cried the wolf, and he swallowed Red Riding Hood right up. Then he crawled back under the covers for a nap.

A short while later, a hunter passed the house and thought, "The old woman is snoring very loudly. I must see if something is wrong."

When he went inside, he found the wolf fast asleep in Grandmother's bed. The hunter was just about to shoot the wolf when he wondered

where the old woman might be. Had the wolf eaten her? The hunter pulled out his knife and cut open the sleeping wolf to check. The first thing he saw was a little red hood, and Red Riding Hood jumped out. Then out climbed her grandmother.

The hunter sent Red Riding Hood to gather some big stones.
Then he filled the wolf with stones and sewed him back up.

The wolf woke up with a belly full of stones.
He tried to roll over. Then he tried to sit.

Finally he managed to get to his feet for
a few seconds. Then he fell down dead.

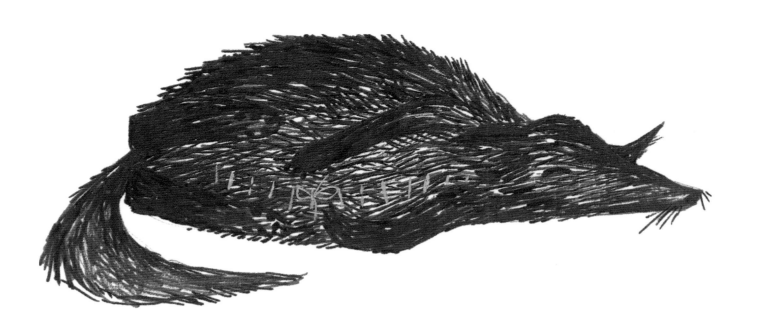

The hunter skinned the wolf and took the skin home to his family.
Grandmother ate the cake and sipped the cordial that Red Riding
Hood had brought, and soon she felt quite strong.

After that, Red Riding Hood often walked to Grandmother's
house—but she never again strayed from the path, and she never,
ever talked to wolves.